DATE DUE

JAN 19 '98	FEB 16 '99	JUN 14 2005
FEB 6 '98	JUN 5 '99	AUG 30 2006
FEB 27 '98	JUN 30 '99	NOV 27 2007
APR 1 '98	AUG 2 '99	JUN 11 2008
APR 17 '98	AUG 27 '99	JUN 27 2008
MAY 5 '98	OCT 18 '99	JAN 26 2009
MAY 23 '98	MAR 31 '00	AUG 26 2010
JUN 16 '98	MAY 17	JUN 15 2011
JUL 8 '98	MAY 30	SEP -5 2012
AUG 4 '98	MAY 31	FEB 2 2013
SEP 4 '98	SEP 26	FEB 22 2013
SEP 23 '98	MAR 9 '01	MAR 16 2013
OCT 12 '98	MAR 23 '01	APR 30 2013
NOV 3 '98	APR 7 '01	MAY 06 2015
NOV 20 '98	APR 7 2003	JUN 1 - 2015
DEC 8 '98	AUG 9 2005	DEC 04 2015
DEC 28 '98	JUN 6 2008	

E
Car   Carlisle, Bob
          Butterfly Kisses

A Special Gift

Presented to

Price James Library

in memory of

Megan Backes

by

Karla, Ross, Carl and Toby

Christmas 1997

Butterfly Kisses

Bob Carlisle

Text adapted by
Cindy Sterling • **Sally Huss**

Illustrated by

Tommy NELSON

Thomas Nelson, Inc.
Nashville

BOB CARLISLE
BUTTERFLY KISSES.

Text Copyright © 1997 by Bob Carlisle.
Illustrations copyright © 1997 by Sally Huss.

Managing Editor: Laura Minchew
Project Editor: Beverly Phillips

Butterfly Kisses written by Bob Carlisle & Randy Thomas
©1996 Diadem Music Publishing & PolyGram International Publishing, Inc.
Used with permission.

Library of Congress Cataloging-in-Publication Data
Sterling, Cindy.
    Butterfly kisses / Bob Carlisle ; text adapted by Cindy Sterling ; illustrated by Sally Huss.
      p.   cm.
    Summary: A father recalls many special times he and his daughter have shared as she grows up.
    ISBN 0-8499-5822-9
    1. Children's songs—United States—Texts.   [1. Fathers and daughters—Songs and music.   2. Songs.]   I. Carlisle, Bob. II. Huss, Sally, ill.   III. Title.
PZ8.3.S825Bu   1997
782.42164'0268—dc21
                                             97-39757
                                              CIP
                                              AC

Printed in the United States of America

97 98 99 00 01 02 LBM 9 8 7 6 5 4 3 2

Butterfly Kisses

There's two things I know for sure.
She was sent here from heaven, and she's
   Daddy's little girl.
As I drop to my knees by her bed at night,
   She talks to Jesus, and I close my eyes.
And I thank God for all of the joy in my life,
But most of all, for . . .

Butterfly Kisses after bedtime prayer.
Stickin' little white flowers all up in her hair.
"Walk beside the pony, Daddy, it's my first ride."
"I know the cake looks funny, Daddy,
   but I sure tried."
Oh, with all that I've done wrong,
   I must have done something right
To deserve a hug every morning
   and Butterfly Kisses at night.

Sweet Sixteen today,
She's looking like her mama
   a little more every day.
One part woman, the other part girl
To perfume and makeup,
   from ribbons and curls.
Trying her wings out in a great big world.
But I remember, our . . .

Butterfly Kisses after bedtime prayer
Stickin' little white flowers all up in her hair.
"You know how much I love you, Daddy,
   but if you don't mind,
I'm only going to kiss you on the cheek
   this time."

With all that I've done wrong,
   I must have done something right
To deserve her love every morning
   And Butterfly Kisses at night.

   All the precious time
   Like the wind, the years go by.
   Precious butterfly
   Spread your wings and fly.

She'll change her name today.
She'll make a promise, and I'll give her away.
Standing in the bride's room, just staring at her,
She asked me what I'm thinking,
   and I said, "I'm not sure."
"I just feel like I'm losing my baby girl."
Then she leaned over and gave me . . .

Butterfly Kisses, with her mama there,
Stickin' little white flowers all up in her hair.
"Walk me down the aisle, Daddy.
   It's just about time."
"Does my wedding gown look pretty, Daddy?"
   "Daddy, don't cry."
With all that I've done wrong,
   I must have done something right
To deserve her love every morning,
   and Butterfly Kisses . . .

   I couldn't ask God for more.
   Man, this is what love is.
   I know I've gotta let her go,
   But I'll always remember . . .
   Every hug in the morning
   and Butterfly Kisses . . .

Written by Bob Carlisle & Randy Thomas
©1996 Diadem Music Publishing & PolyGram International Publishing, Inc.
Used by permission.

you were the tiniest baby. You wiggled and giggled when I held you in my arms. You were my precious daughter, and I loved you from the very beginning. And I thanked God for you.

I fluttered my eyelashes on your warm cheek. You smiled at me and fluttered right back. That's how it started...

Butterfly Kisses.

When you took your first pony ride, you were very brave. But I could tell you were a little afraid and I walked beside you. You held my hand so tightly.

You were always Daddy's little girl.

You were the funniest clown at the costume party. Your red rubber nose fell into the punch. Of all the kids, you laughed the loudest.

On Father's Day you drew a very creative picture of me. And you didn't even get upset when I thought my head was a potato.
You were always so much fun.

You were the prettiest angel in the
Christmas pageant. You sang out
"Glory to God in the Highest!" I had
to give your mom my handkerchief.
I think there were eleven angels, but
I only saw you.

You will always be my angel.

At bedtime we knelt beside your bed, and you talked to Jesus.

Silently I thanked God for you.
And for...

Butterfly

Kisses

On my birthday you baked me this awesome cake with licorice and jelly beans and lots and lots and lots of candles. Growing older never felt so good.

You always made me feel special.

You were the craziest swimmer in the ocean. Birds flew high above your head. Fish swam all around your legs and feet. "What is <u>that</u>?" they wondered. Splashes were everywhere!

You made every day exciting.

At the dance recital, you were the most graceful ballerina. You floated across the stage like a butterfly and landed perfectly on your toes.

When you slid into home plate at the big game, the umpire called you "out." You were the toughest shortstop. You skinned your elbows and choked back tears.
   You always tried your best.

And when all those girls came over for your slumber party, there were funny pillow fights and silly secrets. And lots and lots and _lots_ of giggles.

Because of your new braces, you couldn't chew bubble gum anymore. But you made sure that all the other girls had plenty.
You have always been a great friend.

Several more years flew by and
you weren't a little girl anymore.

I noticed that sometimes your mom let you wear a dab of her perfume. Or borrow her tiny gold earrings. I wasn't ready for you to grow up just yet.
It's always tough for a dad to let go.

Just the other day
I found you in the attic.
You were wearing high-top sneakers,
baggy jeans, and my old high school
football jersey. Your mom's wedding
veil looked like a halo around
your face.

I don't know what you saw in your reflection.

But I saw three girls. One was a Christmas angel. One was a tough shortstop. One was a beautiful young lady who looked a lot like her mom.

I walked over to you, my precious daughter. You smiled and put your arms around me. You fluttered your eyelashes on my damp cheek. And I thanked God for you. And for...

Butterfly
Kisses

I love you.